CAPTAIN UNDERPANTS
Two WEDGIE-
POWERED
Novels in One
FULL COLOUR!

SCHOLASTIC

Published in the UK by Scholastic Children's Books, 2020
Euston House, 24 Eversholt Street, London, NW1 1DB
A division of Scholastic Limited

London – New York – Toronto – Sydney – Auckland
Mexico City – New Delhi – Hong Kong

SCHOLASTIC and associated logos are trademarks and/or
registered trademarks of Scholastic Inc.

Captain Underpants and the Invasion of the Incredibly
Naughty Cafeteria Ladies from Outer Space
first published in the US by Scholastic Inc., 1999.
Copyright © Dav Pilkey, 1999

Captain Underpants and the Perilous Plot of Professor Poopypants
first published in the US by Scholastic Inc., 2000
Copyright © Dav Pilkey, 2000

The right of Dav Pilkey to be identified as the author and illustrator of this work
has been asserted by him under the Copyright, Designs and Patents Act 1988.

ISBN 978 0702 30581 8

A CIP catalogue record for this book is available from the British Library.

Printed in China

3 5 7 9 10 8 6 4 2
This is a work of fiction. Names, characters, places, incidents
and dialogues are products of the author's imagination or are used
fictitiously. Any resemblance to actual people, living or dead, events
or locales is entirely coincidental.

www.scholastic.co.uk

FULL COLOUR

CAPTAIN UNDERPANTS

AND THE INVASION OF THE Incredibly Naughty CAFETERIA Ladies FROM OUTER SPACE (and the Subsequent Assault of The EQUALLY EVIL Lunchroom ZOMBIE Nerds)

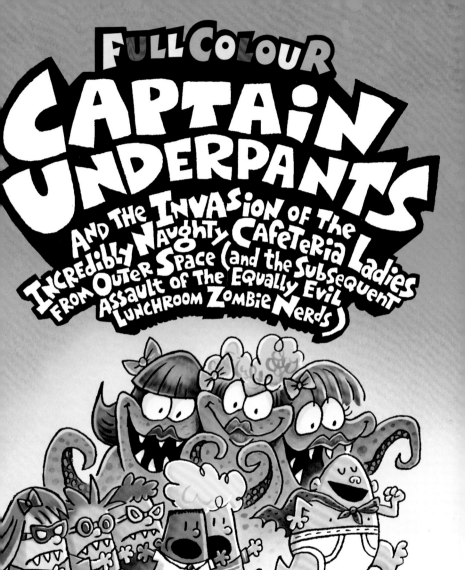

The Third Epic Novel by

DAV PILKEY

with colour by Jose Garibaldi

SCHOLASTIC

For John "Sparky" Johnson

CHAPTERS

George Beard and
Harold Hutchins
present:
A "Deny Everything"
Production

EPISODE 1
the Fantom
Principal

A Long time Ago, in a
Elementary School far
far away...

There were two
cool Kids Named
George and Harold.

WE
rule

ME
TOO

They had a evil
Principle Named
Mr. Krupp, who was
strong in
The ways
of The
FORSE!

Blah
Blah

He FORSED
them to study

Blah Blah Blah

He FORSED
Them to Clean

BLah
BLaH
BLaH

And he FORSED
Them To
BEHAVE!

HA HA
HA!

Now the only way they can turn Captain Under-pants back into MR. KRUPP, is to pour water over his head!

But the worst part is that George and Harold have to keep an eye on Mr. Krupp.

Blah Blah Blah

Because for some **STRANGE** reason, whenever he hears somebody snap there fingers...

SNAP!

...he turns BACK into YOU-KNOW-WHO!

TRA LA LAAA

So whatever you do, **PLEASE DON'T** snap your fingers around Mr. Krupp.

You heard the man! PLEASE PLEASE, PLEASE Don't SNAP Those Fingers!

This has been a public servise Anouncement from George and Harold... who **STILL** deny everything!

CHAPTER 1
GEORGE AND HAROLD

This is George Beard and Harold Hutchins.
George is the kid on the left with the tie
and the flat-top. Harold is the one on the
right with the T-shirt and the bad haircut.
Remember that now.

If you were looking for a few words to describe George and Harold, you might come up with *kind*, *funny*, *smart*, *determined*, and *deep*.

Just ask their principal, Mr. Krupp. He'll tell you that George and Harold are **KIND**a **FUNNY**-lookin' **SMART** alecks who are **DETERMINED** to drive everybody off the **DEEP** end!

But don't listen to him.

George and Harold are actually very clever and good-hearted boys. Their only problem is that they're fourth graders. And at George and Harold's school, fourth graders are expected to sit still and pay attention for *seven hours a day*!

George and Harold are just not very good at that.

The only thing George and Harold *are* good at is being silly. Unfortunately, George and Harold's silliness gets them into trouble every now and then. Sometimes it gets them into a LOT of trouble. And one time it got them into *SO MUCH* trouble, it almost caused the entire Earth to be destroyed by an army of giant evil zombie nerds!

But before I can tell you that story, I have to tell you *this* story . . .

CHAPTER 2
THE EVIL SPACE GUYS

One dark, clear night in Piqua, Ohio, a flaming object was seen streaking across the quiet midnight sky.

It shone brightly for a second or two, then fizzled out just above Jerome Horwitz Elementary School. Nobody gave it a second thought.

The next day, everything seemed pretty normal. Nobody noticed anything different about the school. Nobody paid any attention to the roof. And of course, nobody looked up and said, "Hey, what's that big spaceship thingy doing on the roof of the school?"

Perhaps if they had, the horrible ordeal that followed might never have happened, and you wouldn't be sitting here reading about it right now. But they didn't, it did, and, well, here we are.

As we can all plainly see, there was a spaceship on top of the building. And inside that spaceship were three of the most evil, hideous, and merciless spacemen ever to set foot on the roof of a small midwestern elementary school.

Their names were Zorx, Klax, and Jennifer. Their mission? To take over planet Earth.

"First," said Zorx, "we must find a way to infiltrate the school."

"Then," said Klax, "we will turn all the children into giant, super-powered evil zombie nerds!"

"Finally," said Jennifer, "we will use them to take over the world!" Zorx and Klax laughed and laughed.

"Silence, you fools!" barked Jennifer. "If our plan is to work, we must wait until it is narratively convenient. In the meantime, we will watch their every move on our trinocloscope!"

CHAPTER 3
FUN WITH SCIENCE

Early that same morning, George and Harold were sitting in their 10:15 A.M. science class making silly noises.

"Meeowwwww," George mewed softly, without moving his lips.

"Rrrr-rrr-rrrr," growled Harold, without opening his mouth.

"There it is *again*!" exclaimed their science teacher, Mr. Fyde. "I *distinctly* heard a cat and a dog in here!"

"We didn't hear anything," the children said, trying not to laugh.

"I-I must be *hearing* things again," Mr. Fyde worried.

"Maybe you should leave and go see a doctor," said George with concern.

"I can't," said Mr. Fyde. "Today is the day of the big volcano experiment."

The children all groaned. Mr. Fyde's science experiments were usually the most idiotic things on earth. They almost never worked and were *always* boring.

But today's experiment was different. Mr. Fyde brought in a large, fake-looking volcano that he had made out of papier-mâché. He filled the volcano with a box of ordinary baking soda.

"Baking soda is also called 'sodium bicarbonate,'" explained Mr. Fyde.

"Meeeeowwwwwww."

"Umm . . ." said Mr. Fyde, "did any of you children just hear — umm, uh . . . never mind."

Mr. Fyde opened up a bottle of clear liquid. "Now watch what happens when I pour vinegar into the baking soda," he said.

The children watched as the tiny volcano started to rumble. Soon, a large glob of foamy goop spurted out the top. The goop poured over the desk and dripped onto the floor, creating a huge mess.

"Oops," said Mr. Fyde. "I guess I used too much baking soda."

George and Harold were stunned.

"How did you do that?" asked Harold.

"Well," said Mr. Fyde, "the vinegar acts as a liberating agent, which releases the gaseous carbonate radical element of the sodium bicarbo—"

"Meeeeooowwwwwwww."

"Umm . . . uh," Mr. Fyde paused. "Uh, e-excuse me, children. I-I've got to go and see a doctor."

Mr. Fyde put on his coat and hurried out the door. George and Harold got up and studied the messy volcano experiment with great interest.

"Are you thinking what I'm thinking?" asked George.

"I think I'm thinking what you're thinking," said Harold.

CHAPTER 4
THE SETUP

After school, the two boys raced to
George's house and got down to business.

George and Harold sat down and began
creating a bogus cupcake recipe.

"We'll just add a box of baking soda
and a bottle of vinegar to this recipe," said
George. "And whoever makes these
cupcakes will get a big surprise!"

"Let's add *two* boxes of baking soda and
two bottles of vinegar to the recipe," said
Harold. "That way, they'll get an even
bigger surprise!"

"Good idea!" laughed George.

CHAPTER 5
MR. KRUPP'S KRISPY KRUPCAKES

The next morning at school, George and Harold strolled into the cafeteria and taped a festive-looking card to the kitchen door.

Soon the lunch ladies arrived.

"Oh, look," said Miss Creant, the head lunch lady. "Today is Mr. Krupp's birthday, and he'd like us to make a batch of cupcakes just for him! Isn't that cute?"

"I've got an idea," said the cook, Mrs. DePoint. "Why don't we surprise him and make cupcakes for the *whole school*?!!?"

"Good thinking," said Miss Creant. "Let's see now . . . this recipe serves 10, and we have about 1,000 students and faculty in the school, so . . .

. . . we'll need 100 eggs, 150 cups of flour,
200 boxes of baking soda, 7 quarts of
green food coloring, 50 sticks of butter,
150 cups of sugar — and, let's see . . .
Oh yes, 200 bottles of *vinegar*!"

MR. KRUPP'S KRISPY KRUPCAKES

INGREDIENTS

1 egg
1½ cups of Flour
2 Boxes BAKING Soda
1½ cups SugAR
1 Stick Butter
Green Food Colering
2 Bottles Vinegar

MAKES 10 CUPCAKES

Directions

Mix Flour And SugAR with baking Soda, and egg. Melt butter, Pour into Mixture. Stir in Food Colering. Now Add Vinegar. Mix Well. Pour into Cupcake Thingies. Bake At 45 degrees For 3 hours.

The lunch ladies scurried about,
gathering everything they needed. They
dumped the eggs, food coloring, milk, and
baking soda into a large vat and began to
mix thoroughly.

Then somebody poured in the
vinegar . . .

CHAPTER 6
WHAT HAPPENED NEXT

(Note: Please shake this book back and forth uncontrollably when you read the following word. Also, shout it out as loud as you can. Don't worry, you won't get in trouble.)

"KA-BLOOOOOSH!"

CHAPTER 6½
HERE COMES THE GOOP!

A giant wave of green goop crashed through the cafeteria doors and splashed down the halls, swallowing everything in its path. Book bags, bulletin boards, lunch boxes, coat racks, trophy cases . . . nothing could stand in the way of the gigantic green glob o' goo.

It traveled down the north, east, and west wings of the school, covering everything from the drinking fountains to the text on this page. It squished into lockers, and squashed down the stairs. It billowed into bat____ ____ ____allowed ____

It wasn't long before the green goop
began spilling into all the classrooms.

"Uh-oh," said George. "Something tells
me the lunch ladies made more than just
one batch of Mr. Krupp's Krispy Krupcakes."

"But — but that was *their* idea, not
ours," cried Harold.

"Speaking of *ideas*," said George, "I've
got a good one."

"What?" asked Harold.

"*RUN!*" cried George.

CHAPTER 7
THE WRATH OF THE CAFETERIA LADIES

The next afternoon, as cleaning crews sorted through the sticky green hallways and sticky green classrooms, the cafeteria ladies had a meeting with Mr. Krupp in his sticky green office.

"But it wasn't even my birthday!" cried Mr. Krupp.

"We know you had nothing to do with this!" said Miss Creant. "We think it was those two awful boys, George and Harold!"

"Well, *duh*!" said Mr. Krupp, rolling his eyes. "OF COURSE IT WAS GEORGE AND HAROLD!!! But do you have any proof?"

"PROOF?!!?" said the lunch ladies. "Why, George and Harold are *always* playing tricks on us! Every day, they change the letters around on our lunch sign. They put pepper in the napkin dispensers and unscrew the caps on the saltshakers . . . They start food fights . . . They go sledding on our lunch trays . . . They make everybody laugh so the milk squirts out their noses . . . And they're *constantly creating these awful comic books about us*!!!"

CHAPTER 8
CAPTAIN UNDERPANTS AND THE NIGHT OF THE LIVING LUNCH LADIES

By George Beard
and Harold Hutchins.

CAPTain UNDerpants and the NIGHT OF THE Living LUNCH LADYS

Story By George Beard
Pictures By Harold Hutchins

Late one friday Afternoon, The Lunch Ladys were Cleaning up The CAFFeteria.

There's Lots of half-eaten food in This TRASH Barrel.

Well pour it in and we'll serve it agAin next WEEK!

TRASH

STEW

waste not want not!

TRASH

STEW

But while they were working, The janiter AxidentALLY locked The school for The weekend.

closed

The Lunch Ladys were TRAPped inside!

HELP!

They were forsed to eat there own food To survive.

Past the Lips

Andover The gums..

Look ovt Tummy... Here it Comes.

THEY GOT INTO A BIG FIGHT.

CAPTAIN UNDER-PANTS WAS Faster Than a speeding WAistbAnd...

...More Powerful Than Boxer Shorts...

,And Able to Leap tAll buildings without getting a wedgie.

TRA LA LAAAA

But the Lunch Ladys were Strong Too. They RAn Faster Than Their Runny MeatLOAF GRAVY

They were more Powerful Than The Stench of Their "sloppy-Joe" CassARole

ANd they could Leap TaLL Buildings With The gAssy After-Affects of Their "TexAs-style" chili Con Carney.

B-R-R-R-R-T

Soon they were all on top of a tall building.

We've got you now, waistband warrior!

Not so fast!

Captain Underpants pressed a button on his "Utility Waistband".

click

And out popped a roll of toilet paper.

Even the living dead can't exscape the "Toilet Paper of Justice."

Captain Underpants lassoed the lecherous lunch ladies.

But they had a trick up there sleeves.

Lunch Lady Brand SALSBURY STEAK SAUCE

They poured the steak sauce on the Toilet Paper of Justice.

ssss

CHAPTER 9
QUITTIN' TIME

"We're *fed up* with those two boys!" cried Miss Creant. "They're always making fun of our cooking!"

"Yeah!" said Mrs. DePoint. "Our food isn't *that* bad. I ate here once and hardly got sick at all!"

"Well, I can't punish them if we don't have any proof," said Mr. Krupp.

"Fine!" said the lunch ladies. "Then we *quit*!"

"Ladies, ladies," cried Mr. Krupp. "Be reasonable! You can't just *quit* on such short notice."

But the lunch ladies didn't care. They marched right out of Mr. Krupp's sticky green office, and that was the end of that.

"Rats!" cried Mr. Krupp. "Now where am I going to find three new lunch ladies by tomorrow morning?"

Suddenly there was a knock on Mr. Krupp's door. Three very large women wearing *lots* of makeup walked into his office.

"Hello," said the first woman. "My name is, uh, Zorx*ette*. These are my, uh, sisters, *Klaxette* and, umm, *Jenniferette*. We've come to apply for jobs as cafeteria ladies."

"Wow," said Mr. Krupp. "Do you have any experience?"

"No," said Klaxette.

"Do you have any credentials?" asked Mr. Krupp.

"No," said Zorxette.

"Do you have any references?" asked Mr. Krupp.

"No," said Jenniferette.

"You're hired!" said Mr. Krupp.

"Wonderful," said Jenniferette. "Now our plan to take over the world is — er, I mean, our plan to *feed the children healthy, nutritional meals* is underway!"

The three new lunch ladies laughed horribly. Then they left Mr. Krupp's office and got started preparing the next day's lunch menu.

"Well, *that* was easy," said Mr. Krupp.
"Now to take care of George and Harold!"

CHAPTER 10
BUSTED!

George and Harold were in study hall
when they heard the dreaded announcement
over the intercom:

> "George Beard and Harold Hutchins,
> please report to Mr. Krupp's office
> immediately."

"Oh, no," cried Harold. "We're busted!"
"No way!" said George. "Remember,
what happened yesterday was *not our fault*!
We didn't do it — it was an *accident*!"

But Mr. Krupp was not as understanding. "I can't prove it, but I *know* you boys are responsible for yesterday's disaster," Mr. Krupp said. "I'm going to punish you by taking away your cafeteria privileges for the rest of the year! *No more cafeteria food for you two!*"

"No more cafeteria food?" whispered Harold. "I thought he said he was going to *punish* us."

"Yeah." George smiled. "Maybe if we're *really* bad, he'll take away our *homework* privileges, too!"

"I heard that!" screamed Mr. Krupp. "From now on, you boys are going to have to pack your own lunches and eat in my office so I can keep an eye on you!"

"Rats!" said Harold.

"But we didn't do it!" George protested. "WE DIDN'T DO IT!"

"Too bad, bub!" said Mr. Krupp.

"Boy," said George. "This is probably the first time we've gotten in trouble for something we *didn't* do."

"Unless you count all those times we didn't do our homework," said Harold.

"Oh, yeah," laughed George.

CHAPTER 11
BROWN BAGGIN' IT

The next day, George and Harold each brought their own sandwiches to Mr. Krupp's office for lunch.

"I'll trade you half of my peanut-butter-and-gummy-worm sandwich," said George, "for half of your tuna-salad-with-chocolate-chips-and-miniature-marshmallows sandwich."

"Sure," said Harold. "Y'want some barbecue sauce on that?"

"You kids are DISGUSTING!" Mr. Krupp shouted.

Soon George and Harold were munching on potato chips with whipped cream and chocolate sprinkles. Mr. Krupp was turning green.

"What's for dessert?" asked Harold.

"Hard-boiled eggs dipped in hot fudge and Skittles!" said George.

"AAAUGH!" screamed Mr. Krupp. *"I can't stand it anymore!"* He got up and stumbled out the door for some fresh air.

"You know," said George, "now that Mr. Krupp is gone, we could run to the cafeteria and change the letters around on the lunch sign."

"Cool," said Harold.

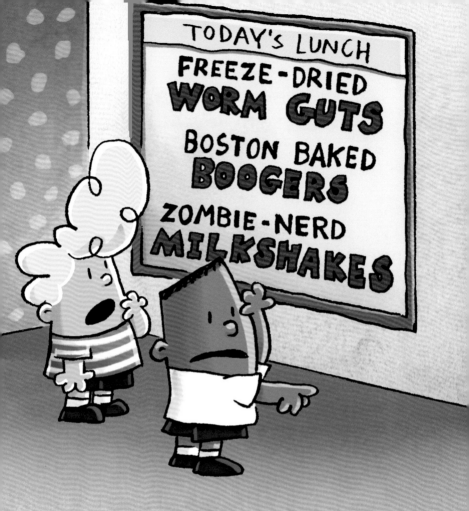

So George and Harold sneaked to the
cafeteria. But when they read the lunch
sign, they were a bit confused.

"What's going on here?" said George.

"It looks like somebody's already
changed the sign," said Harold.

"Forget the sign," said George. "Look
at everybody! *They've* changed!"

It was true. All the kids and teachers in school were entering the cafeteria looking as normal as ever. But they were leaving the cafeteria looking quite different.

"Look!" cried George. "They're all wearing broken eyeglasses held together with masking tape . . . and they've all got vinyl pocket protectors!!! They've all turned into—"

"*Nerds!*" Harold gasped.

"And look at their skin," said George. "They're all gray and clammy. That could only mean one thing!"

"They're — they're ZOMBIE nerds?!!?" asked Harold.

"I'm afraid so," said George.

"Let's just hope they're friendly!" said Harold.

"Whoever heard of a *friendly* zombie nerd?" asked George.

"I'm afraid," Harold whined.

"There's no time to be afraid," said
George. "We've got to get to the bottom
of this!"

"*That's* what I'm afraid of," said Harold.

CHAPTER 12
THE BOTTOM OF THIS

George and Harold crawled into the cafeteria and sneaked through the kitchen doors. There they hid behind a table while the incredibly naughty cafeteria ladies from outer space discussed their plans to take over the world.

"Look at those puny earthlings!" laughed Zorx. "They're all drinking Evil Zombie-Nerd Milkshakes and transforming before our very eyes!"

"It won't be long now," said Klax. "Tomorrow, we'll feed them Super Evil Rapid-Growth Juice! Then they will grow to the size of Xleqxisfp trees."

"Exactly," sneered Jennifer. "Then we will unleash our giant evil zombie nerds upon the earth, and soon the planet will be OURS!"

The three evil space guys threw back their heads and laughed hysterically.

"We've got to tell Mr. Krupp about this," Harold whispered.

"Right," whispered George. "But first, we've got to get rid of that Super Evil Rapid-Growth Juice!

George carefully reached up and swiped the carton of juice.

"What should we do with it?" asked Harold.

"Let's pour it out the window," said George. "That way it won't do any damage."

"Good idea," said Harold.

While the naughty cafeteria ladies continued laughing, George quietly emptied the carton of Super Evil Rapid-Growth Juice out the window.

"You know," whispered Harold, "Mr. Krupp is never going to believe that sinister cafeteria ladies from outer space have turned everybody into evil zombie nerds."

"Sure he'll believe us — he's **GOT** to believe us!" said George. "I *hope* he believes us!"

CHAPTER 13
HE DOESN'T
BELIEVE THEM

"That's the most *ridiculous* story I've ever heard!" laughed Mr. Krupp.

"But it's true!" cried Harold.

"Yeah," said George. "Everybody in the entire school is an evil zombie nerd! The kids, the teachers . . . *everybody*!"

"All right," said Mr. Krupp. "I'll prove it to you!" He pressed the button on his intercom and called for his secretary.

Soon Miss Anthrope entered the room. She was dressed in a pink polka-dot polyester dress, with orthopedic knee-high stockings and ugly brown arch-support loafers.

"See?" said Harold. "She's dressed like a *nerd*!"

"She always dresses like that," snapped Mr. Krupp.

"But she's gray and clammy and reeks of *freakish zombified death*!" cried George.

"She *always smells like that*!" Mr. Krupp argued. "And she's always gray and clammy, too!"

George and Harold had to admit that school secretaries were not very good subjects to compare and contrast with evil zombie nerds.

But then, Miss Anthrope leaned over and took a huge bite out of Mr. Krupp's desk. *"Must destroy Earth,"* she moaned as she took another bite.

Even Mr. Krupp had to agree that Miss Anthrope was acting a bit more evil than usual.

MUNCH
MUNCH

So George and Harold took Mr. Krupp down to the cafeteria to confront the evil lunch ladies.

Suddenly, out of the shadows stepped the evil Zorx. "Gotcha!" Zorx cried, as he grabbed onto Harold's shoulders.

"Aaaagh!" screamed Harold. He squirmed away, pulling Zorx's gloves off and revealing two slimy green tentacles.

"See, Mr. Krupp?" said George. "We told you they were space guys!"

"You FOOLS!" screamed Zorx. "Now we will destroy you!" The evil Zorx pointed his tentacle at George, Harold, and Mr. Krupp, and snapped his fingers:

SNAP!

Suddenly, Mr. Krupp began to change.

A heroic grin spread across Mr. Krupp's face. He threw out his chest and placed his fists firmly at his sides, looking quite triumphant.

"Uh-oh," said George. "That evil space guy just snapped his fingers! Now Mr. Krupp is turning into *you-know-who*!"

"Hey, wait a second," said Harold. "Tentacles don't have fingers! You can't *snap* a tentacle!"

"There's no time to argue the physical improbabilities of this story," said George. "We've got to stop Mr. Krupp from changing into Captain Underpants before it's too late!"

CHAPTER 14
IT'S TOO LATE

Mr. Krupp turned and dashed out the door. His clothes flew off behind him as the hallways echoed with jubilant proclamations about the superiority of underwear.

George and Harold dashed after him, but the door was quickly blocked by Zorx, Klax, and Jennifer.

"You wanna get out of this kitchen," the evil Jennifer mocked, "you gotta go through *US*!"

George grabbed a rolling pin. Harold grabbed a cast-iron frying pan.

"I sure hope we don't have to resort to incredibly graphic violence," said Harold.

"Me, too," said George.

CHAPTER 15
THE INCREDIBLY GRAPHIC VIOLENCE CHAPTER, PART 1 (IN FLIP-O-RAMA™)

WARNING:

The following chapter contains terribly inappropriate scenes that certainly do not belong in a children's book.

If you are offended by such senselessness, please put this book down immediately, raise your arms over your head, and run screaming to your nearest shoe store.

When you get there, ask them to make you a cheeseburger.

(Note: This probably won't help you a bit, but we think it will be funny.)

PILKEY® BRAND
ᴏ-RAMA
HERE'S HOW IT WORKS!

STEP 1
First, place your *left* hand inside the dotted lines marked "LEFT HAND HERE."Hold the book open *flat*.

STEP 2
Grasp the *right-hand* page with your right thumb and index finger (inside the dotted lines marked "RIGHT THUMB HERE").

STEP 3
Now *quickly* flip the right-hand page back and forth until the picture appears to be *animated*.

(For extra fun, try adding your own sound-effects!)

FLIP-O-RAMA 1

(pages 77 and 79)

Remember, flip *only* page 77.
While you are flipping, be sure you
can see the picture on page 77
and the one on page 79.
If you flip quickly, the two
pictures will start to look like
<u>one</u> *animated* picture.

Don't forget to
add your own sound-effects!

LEFT HAND HERE

GEORGE PINS
A PREDATOR.

RIGHT
THUMB
HERE

78

GEORGE PINS
A PREDATOR.

FLIP-O-RAMA 2

(pages 81 and 83)

Remember, flip *only* page 81.
While you are flipping, be sure you
can see the picture on page 81
and the one on page 83.
If you flip quickly, the two
pictures will start to look like
<u>one</u> *animated* picture.

Don't forget to
add your own sound-effects!

LEFT HAND HERE

HAROLD BONKS
A BAD GUY.

RIGHT
THUMB
HERE

HAROLD BONKS
A BAD GUY.

FLIP-O-RAMA 3

(pages 85 and 87)

Remember, flip *only* page 85.
While you are flipping, be sure you
can see the picture on page 85
and the one on page 87.
If you flip quickly, the two
pictures will start to look like
<u>one</u> *animated* picture.

Don't forget to
add your own sound-effects!

LEFT HAND HERE

GEORGE AND HAROLD
SAVE THE DAY!
(FOR NOW)

RIGHT
THUMB
HERE

GEORGE AND HAROLD
SAVE THE DAY!
(FOR NOW)

88

CHAPTER 16
THE ASSAULT OF THE EQUALLY EVIL LUNCHROOM ZOMBIE NERDS

George and Harold had barely caught their breath when Captain Underpants finally showed up.

"Tra-La-Laaaaa!" he said. "I'm here to fight for Truth, Justice, and *all* that is Pre-Shrunk and Cottony!"

"Where were you back in chapter 15 when we needed you?" asked George.

"I was at the shoe store ordering a cheeseburger," said Captain Underpants.

While our three heroes were talking, nobody noticed that Zorx, Klax, and Jennifer had slithered away. The wounded space guys approached the lunchroom loudspeakers and called for their evil zombie nerds.

"Zombie nerds!" instructed Jennifer. "Destroy Captain Underpants—and his little friends, too!"

Soon, every evil zombie nerd in the entire school put down their *Omni* magazines and headed for the cafeteria.

"*Must destroy Underpants,*" they
groaned. "*Must destroy Underpants!*"

Suddenly, our three heroes were
surrounded by evil, vicious zombie
nerds. Closer and closer they came.

"Oh, no!" cried George. "What do we
do now?"

"To the Underwear Cave!" shouted
Captain Underpants.

"There *is* no *Underwear Cave*!" said
Harold.

"Really?" said Captain Underpants. "Well,
let's just climb up that ladder instead."

George, Harold, and Captain
Underpants scurried up the ladder, and
soon they were all on the roof.

"Well, we're safe now," said Harold.

"Yep," said George.

"That's for sure," said Captain
Underpants.

CHAPTER 17
OH, YEAH?

It didn't take long before George, Harold, and Captain Underpants looked behind them.

"Hey," said Harold. "What's that big spaceship thingy doing on the roof of the school?"

"And where did that *super evil rapidly growing* dandelion come from?" asked Captain Underpants.

George and Harold gasped. They looked at each other with the sudden panicked realization that only children who have accidentally created a giant mutated garden nuisance would know.

"Er —" stammered George. "We have *no idea* how *that* happened."

"Er — *yeah*," said Harold. "Absolutely *no idea* at all!"

At that moment, the door to the roof swung open. Zorx poked his evil head out and shouted, "We've got you now!"

With no place else to run, our three heroes quickly scurried up the ladder of the big spaceship thingy and closed the door behind them.

Inside the spaceship, George, Harold, and Captain Underpants discovered a refrigerator filled with strange juices.

"Look," said George. "Here's a carton of Anti-Evil Zombie Nerd Juice. How convenient!"

"And look at this," said Harold. "A carton of Ultra Nasty Self-Destruct Juice. Now *this* could come in handy!"

"And look what I've found," said Captain Underpants. "A whole carton of Extra-Strength Super Power Juice!"

"Hey, gimme that!" said George, snapping the carton out of Captain Underpants's hands.

CHAPTER 18
SPACE CAPTIVES

Suddenly, the door of the spaceship swung open, and the three evil space guys slithered inside.

"Step away from the refrigerator!" screamed Jennifer. "And get into that jail cell!"

George and Harold hid their juice cartons behind their backs, and our three heroes stepped quickly into the jail cell.

Zorx started up the engines and the spaceship lifted off. It rose a few hundred feet in the air and hovered over the school.

"You three puny earthlings are very fortunate," said Jennifer. "You will get to witness the destruction of your planet from the safety of your jail cell. Afterward, you will have the honor of being our obedient space captives!"

"Aw, *man*!" said George and Harold.

"Quickly, Klax," said Jennifer. "Get me a carton of Super Evil Rapid-Growth Juice from the refrigerator. We can pour it into our spray gun and shower it upon our evil zombie nerds!"

CHAPTER 19
THE BIG SWITCHEROO

Klax returned with a carton of Super Evil Rapid-Growth Juice, and placed it on the control panel.

"*Soon*," said Jennifer, "Earth will be *OURS*!"

The three aliens threw back their heads and laughed and laughed.

Suddenly, George got an idea.

He whispered to Harold for a second
or two, then he quietly reached through
the bars of the jail cell and swiped Klax's
carton of Super Evil Rapid-Growth Juice.

George carefully peeled the label off the
carton, and stuck it over the label of his
Ultra Nasty Self-Destruct Juice.

While he was busy doing that, Harold
reached through the bars and switched the
labels of the spray gun and the fuel tank.

Finally, George reached back through the bars and put his carton of Ultra Nasty Self-Destruct Juice (which now read Super Evil Rapid-Growth Juice) on the control panel.

"I don't get it," whispered Captain Underpants. "The fuel tank now says SPRAY GUN, and the spray gun now says FUEL TANK, and the rapid-growth juice has been replaced with self-destruct juice . . . What's it all mean?"

"You'll find out," said Harold, sadly.

102

When the three evil space guys had finished laughing triumphantly, Jennifer reached for the carton that read Super Evil Rapid-Growth Juice and poured it into the nozzle that read SPRAY GUN.

"Oh, I get it," said Captain Underpants. "That space guy didn't pour growth juice into the spray gun—he poured self-destruct juice into the *fuel tank*!"

"Yep," George said sadly.

"And that means this spaceship thingy is going to explode into millions of pieces!"

"Right," said Harold gloomily.

The spaceship began to sputter and shake as smoke billowed out of the control panels. Soon sparks were flying and ceiling tiles were falling.

Captain Underpants smiled proudly because he had figured out George's plan. But his smile didn't last long.

"Hey," he cried. "*WE'RE* in the spaceship thingy! What's gonna happen to *us?*"

"We had to sacrifice ourselves to save the world," said George. "I'm afraid we're not going to make it."

"*Of course* we'll make it," cried Captain Underpants. "We've got *Wedgie Power* on our side!"

CHAPTER 20
THE GREAT ESCAPE

Captain Underpants grabbed a roll of toilet paper from the jail cell lavatory.

"We can swing to safety on *this*!" he said.

"You can't *swing* on toilet paper," said Harold.

"Sure I can," said Captain Underpants. "I just did it in my last comic book!"

Captain Underpants opened the jail cell
window and tossed the toilet paper into a
tall tree below them. "Come on, fellas," he
said. "Let's swing out of here before this
spaceship explodes!"

"That toilet paper won't hold you," said
George. "It's not strong enough!"

"Sure it is," said Captain Underpants.
"It's *two-ply*!"

George and Harold grabbed Captain Underpants's cape. "Don't jump!" they cried.

But Captain Underpants wouldn't listen. He jumped out the window with George and Harold still clinging to his cape.

"AAAAAAAAAAAAAAHGH!" they screamed as they fell to the ground and were killed instantly.

Just kidding.

Of course the toilet paper could not support the weight of our three heroes, and for a moment it looked like they were doomed.

But suddenly, Captain Underpants's red polyester cape opened up like a parachute— *PHOOOOP!*

George, Harold, and the Waistband Warrior floated down safely as the spaceship above them exploded.

KA-BOOM!

"Hallelujah!" cried Harold. *"We're not gonna die!* WE'RE NOT GONNA DIE!"

"Or . . ." said George. "Maybe we *are*."

CHAPTER 21
THE DELIRIOUSLY DANGEROUS DEATH-DEFYING DANDELION OF DOOM

George, Harold, and Captain Underpants floated downward, directly into the waiting jaws of the Dandelion of Doom.

"Aw, *man*!" cried Harold. "We *could* have gotten killed in a cool exploding spaceship. But instead, we're gonna get eaten by a *dandelion*. How *humiliating*!"

"Yeah," George moaned. "People are going to be giggling at our funerals."

The dandelion munched Captain Underpants and swung George and Harold around like a couple of rag dolls.

The two boys flew off and landed on the roof of the school.

"HELP MEEEeeEEEEeeEEEeeeEEE," screamed Captain Underpants as the Dandelion of Doom swung him back and forth.

"What should we do?" cried Harold.

"I've got an idea," said George. "It's a bad idea, and I know we're going to regret it, but we've got to act fast! The fate of the entire planet is in our hands."

The next time the giant evil dandelion lurched toward the boys, George poured some Extra-Strength Super Power Juice into Captain Underpants's mouth.

"What do you think is going to happen now?" asked Harold.

"I don't know," said George. "But I have a feeling it's gonna involve incredibly graphic violence!"

CHAPTER 22
THE INCREDIBLY GRAPHIC VIOLENCE CHAPTER, PART 2 (IN FLIP-O-RAMA™)

WARNING:

The following chapter contains **scenes of a very unpleasant nature.**

All nastiness was performed by a qualified stuntman and a licensed stuntplant. Do not attempt to battle giant evil dandelions at home, even if you have recently consumed Extra-Strength Super Power Juice.

Such behavior could result in serious boo-boos.

—The National Board of Boo-Boo Prevention

FLIP-O-RAMA 4

(pages 117 and 119)

Remember, flip *only* page 117.
While you are flipping, be sure you
can see the picture on page 117
and the one on page 119.
If you flip quickly, the two
pictures will start to look like
<u>one</u> *animated* picture.

Don't forget to
add your own sound-effects!

LEFT HAND HERE

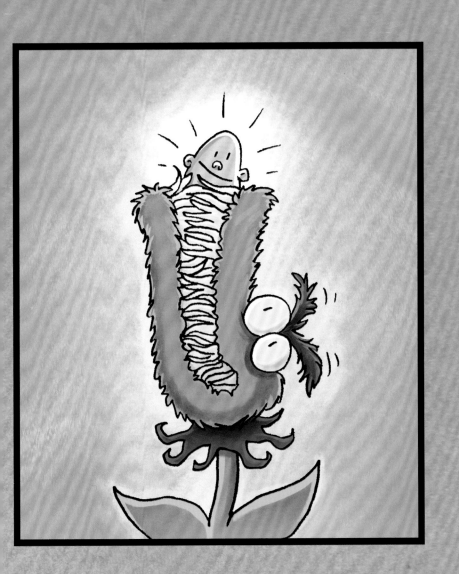

WHEN DANDELIONS ATTACK

117

RIGHT
INDEX
FINGER
HERE

118

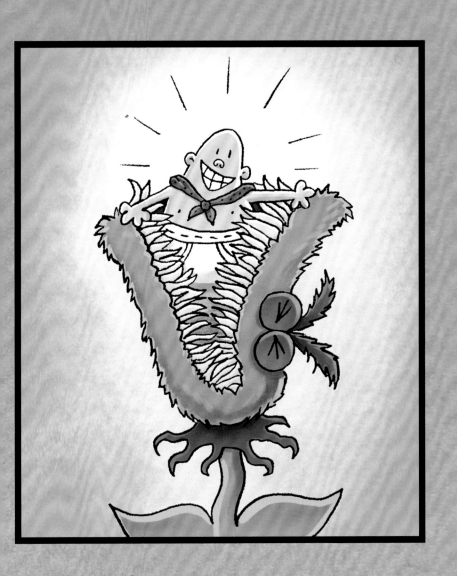

WHEN DANDELIONS
ATTACK

FLIP-O-RAMA 5

(pages 121 and 123)

Remember, flip *only* page 121.
While you are flipping, be sure you
can see the picture on page 121
and the one on page 123.
If you flip quickly, the two
pictures will start to look like
<u>one</u> *animated* picture.

Don't forget to
add your own sound-effects!

LEFT HAND HERE

THE WEDGIE
WEED WHACKER

THE WEDGIE
WEED WHACKER

FLIP-O-RAMA 6

(pages 125 and 127)

Remember, flip *only* page 125.
While you are flipping, be sure you
can see the picture on page 125
and the one on page 127.
If you flip quickly, the two
pictures will start to look like
<u>one</u> *animated* picture.

Don't forget to
add your own sound-effects!

LEFT HAND HERE

HOORAY FOR
CAPTAIN
UNDERPANTS!

RIGHT
THUMB
HERE

RIGHT
INDEX
FINGER
HERE

126

HOORAY FOR CAPTAIN UNDERPANTS!

CHAPTER 23
THE TWENTY-THIRD CHAPTER

Captain Underpants (with the help of his newly developed super powers) had defeated the deliriously dangerous death-defying Dandelion of Doom! Now the only thing left to do was to stop the evil zombie nerds.

"Oh, *HOW* are we going to conquer the evil zombie nerds?" asked George. "How will we ever change them back to normal?"

"Well, we could try this Anti-Evil Zombie Nerd Juice," said Harold.

George rolled his eyes. "I was hoping for something a *little* more dramatic," he said, "but we're running out of pages. Let's do it."

So Harold mixed up a batch of Anti-Evil Zombie Nerd Root Beer, and ordered everybody in the school to drink some.

The evil zombie nerds lined up. "Must drink root beer," they moaned. "Must drink root beer."

When the last zombie nerd had swallowed
his last sip of root beer, George ordered
Captain Underpants to get dressed back up
like Mr. Krupp.

"But I'll lose my super powers if I put
on clothing," said Captain Underpants.
"The power of underwear must be—"

"Just put the clothes on, bub!" George
instructed.

Captain Underpants did as he was told, and then George poured water over the hero's head.

"Now all we can do is wait," said Harold. "Wait and hope that everybody returns to normal."

CHAPTER 24
TO MAKE A LONG STORY SHORT

They did.

CHAPTER 25
BACK TO NORMAL?

"Hooray," said Harold. "It's great to have everybody back to normal."

"Yep," said George. "That's for sure."

But "back to normal" probably wasn't the best choice of words. For while the students and faculty were the same as they'd always been, something had definitely *changed* about Mr. Krupp.

Because from that day on, whenever he heard the sounds of fingers snapping . . .

SNAP!

. . . Mr. Krupp not only turned back into you-know-who, but he also had *Extra-Strength Super Powers*.

And if you thought it was hard for
George and Harold to keep up with him
before, well . . .

. . . you ain't seen nothin' yet!

"OH, NO!" screamed Harold.

"HERE WE GO AGAIN!" screamed George.

Tree
HOUSE
comix
iNc.
Presents

DOG MaN
and The wrath of Petey

Action

Drama

Laffs

a epic novella by
George Beard and
Harold Hutchins

3

4

5

6

meanwhile, DOG man was Hiding in a alley

munch munch

Trash can

Then...

📰 NEWS ✦

PETEY RUNS amuck

BUT where is DOG man huh?

Trash can

DOG man Felt ashamed.

He knew he must Be Brave

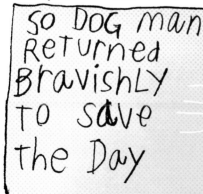

So DOG man Returned BRavishLy To Save the Day

DOG MAN DUG all the way under the Zoo.

nks   HIPPO   LiON   eLephant

He came up in the skunk cage.

SSSS   SSSSS

11

Petey Ran Out Of The Hole

Right Into a Cop's Net

got-cha

You're going to Jail, Buster

rats!

FLIP-O-rama

Here's How 2 do it.

Put your Left Hand There on dotted Line

Hold the other page with your thumb

Flip the page Back and Forth

It makes it look Like a moving cartoon

12

Left Hand Here

Bathtime
for
Dog man

RIGHT
THUMB
HERE

13

Bathtime
For
Dog man

FUN FACTS

FUN FACT #1

Dav Pilkey never ate cafeteria food as a kid. He went to small parochial schools that didn't have lunch programs, so he carried his lunch in a super-cool *Planet of the Apes* metal lunch box. Dav got his first taste of cafeteria food when he became a writer and began visiting elementary schools. Sometimes the food tasted OK, and other times it was pretty nasty, but it always smelled the same: kind of a combination of hamburger grease, diapers, and musty beach towels, with just a slight whiff of burned plastic. He began to wonder what made the food smell that way. What if it was some sort of alien plot to control the brains of children? This idea was his inspiration for the third Captain Underpants book.

FUN FACT #2

Xleqxisfp trees are over 700 feet tall and smell like raisin bread (though they taste kinda like chicken).

FUN FACT #3

Dav no longer thinks that cafeteria food is an alien conspiracy to control the minds of children. Now he thinks it's a government conspiracy.

FULL COLOUR
CAPTAIN UNDERPANTS
AND THE PERILOUS PLOT OF
Professor Poopypants

The Fourth Epic Novel by

DAV ~~Pilkey~~

GIDGET AMSTERBRAINS

with colour by Jose Garibaldi

SCHOLASTIC

CHAPTERS

THE TOP-SECRET TRUTH ABOUT CAPTAIN UNDERPANTS

ALL NEW

Once upon a time there were two cool kids named George and Harold.

we are Awesome

me too.

they had a mean old principle named MR. Krupp.

Blah Blah Blah!

Mr. Krupp was very mean to George and Harold.

Blah Blah Blah

So they bought the 3-D Hypno Ring.

They used it to Hypnotise Mr. Krupp.

you will obey us

Okey Dokey

But They Made A Terible Misteak.

You Are now CAPTAIN UNDERpantS

HA· HA

O.K.

Hey! come bACK MR. KRUpp!

TRA-LA LAAAA

MR. KRUPP Thought he realy WAS CAPTAIn Underpants... But he dident have Any Super powers.

stop

You big dummy

They hAD a Lot of advenchers. One time They even got ATTACKED BY A U.F.O. !!!

UH-OH!

They ALL got Took into The space ship... And George stole Some ALien "Super power Juice".

Then Mr. Krupp got Eaten by A big evil DandyLion.

...you Had to be there.

So George gave him Some "Super power Juice"

TreeHousE comix
INC.

CHAPTER 1
GEORGE AND HAROLD

This is George Beard and Harold Hutchins. George is the kid on the left with the tie and the flat-top. Harold is the one on the right with the T-shirt and the bad haircut. Remember that now.

All of the "experts" at Jerome Horwitz Elementary School had their opinions about George and Harold. Their guidance counselor, Mr. Rected, thought the boys suffered from A.D.D. The school psychologist, Miss Labler, diagnosed them with A.D.H.D. And their mean old principal, Mr. Krupp, thought they were just plain old *B.A.D.*!

But if you ask me, George and Harold simply suffered from I.B.S.S. (Incredibly Boring School Syndrome).

You see, George and Harold weren't really bad kids. They were actually very bright, good-natured boys. Their only problem was that they were bored in school. So they took it upon themselves to "liven things up" for everybody. Wasn't that thoughtful of them?

Unfortunately, George and Harold's *thoughtfulness* got them into trouble every now and then. Sometimes it got them into a *LOT* of trouble. And one time it got them into *so much* trouble, it almost caused the entire planet to be taken over by a ruthless, maniacal, mad-scientist guy in a giant robot suit!

But before I can tell you that story, I have to tell you *this* story . . .

CHAPTER 2
ALL HAIL
NEW SWISSLAND

As everybody knows, New Swissland is a small country just southeast of Greenland. You probably know all about New Swissland's natural resources and systems of government. But here's something about New Swissland that I'll bet you didn't know: Everybody in New Swissland has a silly name.

Just ask their president, the Honorable Chuckles Jingleberry McMonkeyburger Jr. or his lovely wife, Stinky.

They'll tell you all about New Swissland's proud "silly name" heritage. They'll tell you about the cultural significance of silly names. And then they'll probably tell you a really, really long, boring story of how this stupid tradition got started. We'll skip that part, OK?

Just remember that everybody in New Swissland has a silly name. From the richest to the poorest, from the dumbest to the smartest.

And speaking of the *smartest*, let me introduce you to Professor Pippy P. Poopypants. That's a statue of him down there in the bottom right-hand corner of the page. Now, Pippy P. Poopypants was probably the smartest person in all of New Swissland. He graduated at the head of his class at Chunky Q. Boogernose University, and afterward spent all of his time creating wild and fantastic inventions.

Let's look in on him, shall we?

iPPER Q. PPERDRiPPER

IVANA GODA de' BAFROOM

PROFESSOR PiPPY P. POOPYPANTS

Back in his private laboratory, Professor Pippy P. Poopypants was just putting the finishing touches on two wonderful new inventions: the Shrinky-Pig 2000, and the Goosy-Grow 4000.

Professor Poopypants called for his assistant, Porkbelly Funkyskunk. "Mr. Funkyskunk," Pippy yelled, "I am now ready to test my new inventions!"

Porkbelly took notes while the professor aimed his Shrinky-Pig 2000 at a hideous pile of trash.

BLLLLLLZZZZRRRRK!

A powerful beam of energy blasted the garbage heap. Suddenly, the large pile of trash shrank to the size of a gumball.

"Hooray! It works!" cried Professor Poopypants. "Now I must try the Goosy-Grow 4000."

Pippy and Porkbelly aimed the
Goosy-Grow 4000 at an ordinary hot dog
with mustard.

GGGGLLUUZZZZZZZZRRRRRT! went
another bright beam of energy.

Suddenly, the hot dog grew and grew until it crashed through the walls of the laboratory.

"We did it!" exclaimed Porkbelly.

"What do you mean, *WE*?!!?" yelled Professor Poopypants. "*I* did it! *I'm* the GENIUS! You're just a lowly assistant—and don't you forget it!"

"Sorry, boss," said Porkbelly.

"With these two inventions," exclaimed Professor Poopypants, "I will be able to solve the world's garbage problem AND create enough food for everyone on the entire planet!"

Finally, it looked as if all of the Earth's dilemmas would be fixed forever. But who would have believed that in just a few short weeks, Professor Poopypants would be trying to take over the planet in a fit of frenzied rage?

Well, dear readers, the tragic tale is about to unfold. But before I can tell you that story, I have to tell you *this* story . . .

CHAPTER 3
THE FIELD TRIP

Jerome Horwitz Elementary School was having its big annual field trip to Piqua Pizza Palace. All of the kids had brought their permission slips and were lined up to get on the bus. George and Harold could hardly wait to eat pizza and play video games all afternoon.

"This is gonna RULE!" said George.

"Yeah, if we ever get there," said Harold.

"Hey," said George, "let's change the letters around on the school sign while we're waiting."

"Good idea," said Harold.

JEROME HORWITZ ELEMENTA

PIZZA PALACE
FIELD TRIPS
ARE TODAY

So George and Harold ran over to the
sign and began their, um, *thoughtfulness*.
Unfortunately, the boys didn't notice a
dark, foreboding presence lurking nearby
in the bushes.

"A-HA!" cried Mr. Krupp. "I caught you boys *red-handed*!"

"Uh-oh!" said George.

"Heh-heh," laughed Harold. "Th-This is just a little joke."

"A *JOKE*?!!?" yelled Mr. Krupp. "Do you boys think that's funny???"

George and Harold thought for a moment. "Well . . . *yeah*," said George.

"Don't *you*?" asked Harold.

"*NO*, I don't think it's funny!" yelled Mr. Krupp. "I think it's rude and offensive!"

"That's why it's funny," said George.

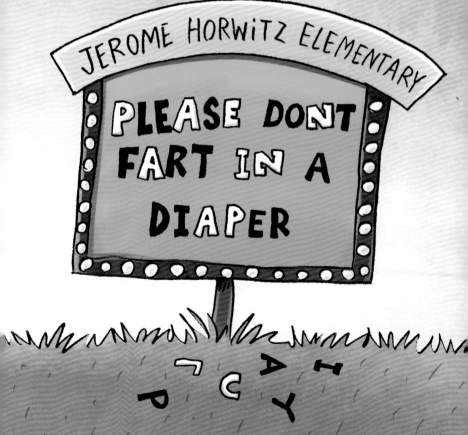

JEROME HORWITZ ELEMENTARY

PLEASE DONT FART IN A DIAPER

"*Oh*," said Mr. Krupp. "You boys like to laugh, huh? Well, here's a good one: You two are officially *BANNED* from the school field trip! Instead of eating pizza, you'll spend the afternoon cleaning up the teachers' lounge! Isn't *that* funny?!!?"

"No way!" said Harold.

"That's not funny at all," said George. "That's cruel and unusual punishment."

"*That's why it's funny!*" Mr. Krupp snarled.

CHAPTER 4
LEFT BEHIND

Mr. Krupp marched George and Harold
over to the janitor's closet.

"You can use these supplies to clean
the teachers' lounge," said Mr. Krupp. "I
want it SPOTLESS by the time we get back!"

Mr. Krupp went back outside, climbed
onto the school bus, and laughed loudly
as the buses pulled away. The teachers
all pointed at George and Harold and
laughed, too.

"Rats!" said Harold. "I thought we were
going to have *fun* today!"

"We can still have fun," said George. "All we need is this ladder, that bag of powdered paste, and those big boxes of Styrofoam wormy thingies."

So George and Harold carried their supplies to the teachers' lounge and got down to business.

At the sink, George pulled the sprayer nozzle, while Harold carefully taped the sprayer handle in the "on" position.

Then the two boys put the nozzle back, making sure the sprayer head was pointed in the right direction.

Next, George held the ladder steady while Harold climbed up to the ceiling fan. There he began scooping generous amounts of powdered paste onto the tops of the fan blades.

"Is this right?" asked Harold.

"Yeah," said George. "Try to get most of it on the *ends* of the blades."

"Got it," said Harold.

George closed all the blinds while
Harold adjusted the ceiling fan so it would
turn on when the lights came on. Finally,
the boys filled the refrigerator up with
worm-shaped Styrofoam packaging pellets.

"This is going to be *fun*," said Harold.

"Not for the teachers!" laughed George.

192

CHAPTER 5
THE FUN BEGINS

An hour or so later, the buses returned to the school. All of the children got off, packed up their stuff, and got ready to go home.

Mr. Fyde, the science teacher, was on school bus duty. The rest of the teachers gathered around George and Harold and began teasing them.

"You kids sure did miss a *FUN* field trip!" said Ms. Ribble. "The pizza was *SO* delicious! Too bad *you* didn't get any!"

"I wanted to bring you back a pizza," said Mr. Meaner, "but I ate it on the bus!" He threw an empty pizza box at George and Harold's feet, and the teachers howled with laughter.

"Maybe you can lick the cheese off the box," Mr. Krupp roared.

The teachers eventually got tired of taunting George and Harold, so they retreated to the teachers' lounge to relax.

"Hey, how come it's so dark in here?" asked Mr. Meaner, as he flicked on the lights. The ceiling fan began rotating very slowly . . .

Ms. Ribble went to the sink and turned on the faucet. Suddenly, the spray nozzle sprayed cold water all over her.

"AAAAUGH!" she screamed. "Somebody turn the water off!" The other teachers sprang up and tried to help. They all got sprayed, too.

The ceiling fan was rotating faster now, and some of the powdered paste had begun flying off the fan blades.

The teachers struggled with the faucet, pushing and shoving each other. Finally, somebody turned the water off . . . but not before everyone was thoroughly *SOAKED*!

The ceiling fan was now spinning at full speed. All of the powder on the fan blades had been flung off, and it was now floating down onto the wet teachers.

"Hey, what the—" cried Mr. Meaner.

"What's all this sticky stuff?!!?" yelled Miss Anthrope.

By now, all of the teachers were covered in gooey, sticky paste. It didn't take a genius to know that George and Harold were behind all this.

"Those brats better not have touched my diet soda!" Ms. Ribble shouted. She dashed to the refrigerator and swung the door open.

SWISH!

Suddenly, thousands of tiny Styrofoam pellets flew out into the room. The wind from the ceiling fan blew the pellets around and around.

Naturally, they landed on the stickiest things in the room: *the teachers*!

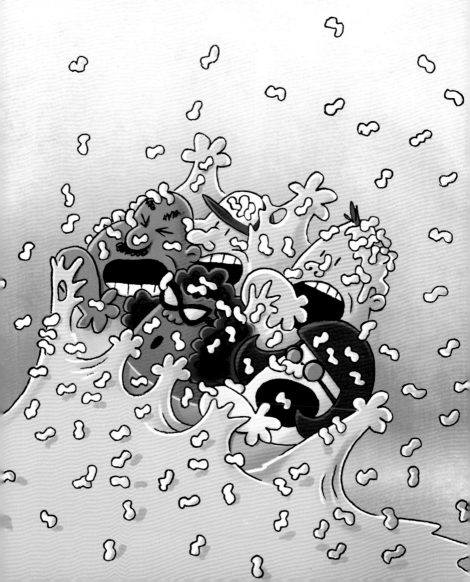

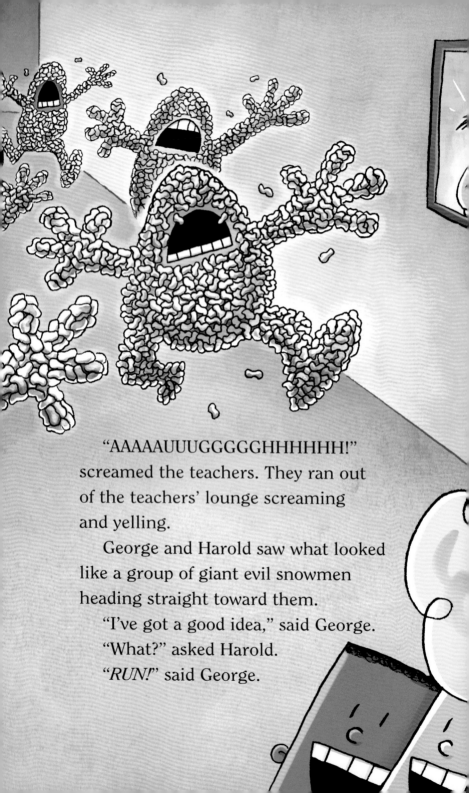

"AAAAAUUUGGGGGHHHHHH!" screamed the teachers. They ran out of the teachers' lounge screaming and yelling.

George and Harold saw what looked like a group of giant evil snowmen heading straight toward them.

"I've got a good idea," said George.

"What?" asked Harold.

"*RUN!*" said George.

CHAPTER 6
BYE-BYE, MR. FYDE

The next day, George and Harold's science teacher, Mr. Fyde, knocked on Mr. Krupp's door.

"What do you want?" barked Mr. Krupp.

"I've—I've come to resign," said Mr. Fyde. "I—I just can't take it anymore."

"Now hold on, bub," said Mr. Krupp. "Being a teacher is hard work! You can't just quit your job when things aren't—"

"You don't understand," said Mr. Fyde. "I think I'm cracking up!"

"What do you mean?" asked Mr. Krupp.

"Well," said Mr. Fyde. "It all started a few months ago when I had this dream that I got eaten up by a talking toilet. Then I started hearing cats and dogs meowing and growling in the classroom. Then, I imagined that the school got flooded with sticky green goop . . . and just yesterday, I thought I saw a group of abominable snowmen chasing two boys down the hallway."

"Now wait just a minute, Morty," said Mr. Krupp. "All of that can be explained."

"—And a few days ago," said Mr. Fyde, "I thought I saw a big fat bald guy in his underwear fly out the window."

"Holy *cow*!" said Mr. Krupp. "You *ARE* crazy!"

So Mr. Fyde handed in his resignation, and left Jerome Horwitz Elementary School for the greener pastures of the Piqua Valley Home for the Reality-Challenged.

"Now, where am I going to find a new science teacher on such short notice?" said Mr. Krupp. "Where, oh where?"

CHAPTER 7
HERE, OH HERE

Remember that Poopypants guy I was telling you about back in chapter 2? Well, things hadn't been going too well for him in the past several weeks.

Professor Poopypants had come to America to share the Shrinky-Pig 2000 and the Goosy-Grow 4000 with the world. But nobody seemed to want to hear about his inventions. They were all too busy . . .

. . . laughing at his silly name.

Poor Pippy Poopypants had been laughed out of every major scientific institution in the U.S. He'd been giggled out of Georgetown, howled out of Harvard, yuk-yukked out of Yale, snickered out of Stanford, and chuckled out of Chattanooga State Technical Community College.

Professor Poopypants was running out of money, and there was no place left for him to turn. Then, one day, the professor walked into a New York coffee shop and picked up a newspaper. And like a message from heaven, Pippy P. Poopypants found his answer.

"THAT'S IT!" he cried. "I'll become an elementary school science teacher!"

"I'll work really hard, and soon, people
will come to respect me and see what a
genius I am. *Then* I can introduce my
great inventions to the world!"

Pippy Poopypants was certain that the
one place people *wouldn't* laugh at his
name was at an elementary school. "Kids
are so accepting and loving," he said. "You
can always count on the sweetness and
innocence of children!"

CHAPTER 8
THE SWEETNESS AND INNOCENCE OF CHILDREN

"Hello, boys and girls," said the professor a week later. "I'm going to be your new science teacher. My name is . . .

"Alright, settle down, boys and girls. Yes, yes, it's a funny name, I know, but let me explain how I got this name. Please, children, settle down. It's not that funny, let me assure you. Um . . . boys and girls . . . BOYS AND GIRLS! Please stop laughing! Alright, I'm going to count to ten, and when I'm done, I want all of you to quiet down so we can learn about the wonderful world of science. One, two, three, four, five, six, seven . . . eight . . . nine . . .

. . . nine and a half . . . ummm. Children, PLEASE STOP LAUGHING! I know you're all very far behind in your lessons, and we've got a lot of catching up to do. Boys and girls! STOP IT! I'm not going to tell you again! IT'S NOT FUNNY! There's no reason at all for you to be laughing at my name! I'm sure we *all* have funny names if you think about it. STOP IT RIGHT NOW! OK, boys and girls, I'll just wait until you all settle down. I can wait . . ."

A week later, things hadn't gotten any better. Professor Poopypants was really beginning to get angry.

"How am I going to get through to these children?" he asked himself. "Hey! I've got it! I'll create a wonderful new invention!"

CHAPTER 9
THE GERBIL JOGGER 2000

The next morning, Professor Poopypants came to school with an odd-looking miniature robot.

"Look, children," he said. "I've created a new invention using the principles of science! I call it the Gerbil Jogger 2000."

The children stopped laughing for a moment and looked with interest at Professor Poopypants's new invention.

"You see, children," said the professor, "some people like to jog, and their pets like to jog along beside them. That's fine if you have a dog or a cat, but what if you have a pet gerbil? It used to be a big problem, but not anymore!"

Professor Poopypants opened the glass dome on the Gerbil Jogger 2000 and inserted a cute, fuzzy gerbil.

The gerbil pushed his tiny legs
against the simple controls, and suddenly
the machine came to life. In no time at
all, the gerbil was jogging around the
classroom in his robot suit. The children
were delighted!

"Wow!" said Connor Mancini. "Science
is COOL!" All of the other children agreed.

This is wonderful! thought Professor
Poopypants. *I've REACHED them! Now I
can TEACH them!*

"Um, excuse me," said George to the
professor. "What's your *middle* name?"

"My middle name," said the professor
proudly, "is *Pee-Pee*. Why do you ask?"

217

At that point, the children picked up
where they had left off: laughing at
Professor Pippy *Pee-Pee* Poopypants's
ridiculous name.

The professor began to shake with
anger. Tiny veins in his forehead started
growing, and his face turned bright red.
"I can't take much more of this," the
furious professor said through clenched
teeth. "I think I might blow a fuse if *just
one more thing* happens!"

CHAPTER 10
JUST ONE MORE THING

Soon afterward, in reading class, the children all heard the story of the Pied Piper of Hamelin.

"You know," said George, "that story gives me an idea!"

So George and Harold began working on their newest comic book: *Captain Underpants and the Pied Pooper of Piqua*.

That afternoon, they snuck into the office and ran off copies of their new adventure to sell on the playground. And everything would have been just fine if one of the third graders hadn't left his copy lying around in the hallway.

CAPTAIN UNDERPANTS
AND THE PIED POOPER OF PIQUA

Story By George Beard • Pictures by Harold Hutchin

Onse upon a time in the city of PIQUA, OHIO, there was A science Teacher Whose name was Pippy PoopyPants

> my middel name is Pee-Pee.

Everybody LaFFed at his funny name.

> HaHaHaHa!

this made PIPPY **MAD!**

> I'LL show them!

So He BILT An Army of Girble Jogger Two Thousends.

> HAHA

He PUT A Girbles in each one

> Hey, MAN!

But He couldent make Them do Any **EVIL STUFF.**

> RATS!

TAP TAP

Then he thought of a evil plan!

BUT OF CORSE!

He made a bunch of Little Headphones and put them on the gerbils.

HEY

Soon, Professor poopypantses army of girbel jogger two thousends were off on a evil RAMPAGE.

They all headed straight for the school!

HAHAHAHAH

Help! The Girble Jogger two thousends broke in the caffateria. They just knocked over some cupcakes and now there attacking the gym teacher!

Quick--- Somebody save the cupcakes!

...MORE POWERFUL Than Boxer Shorts...

OWIE!

...And Abel To LEAP Tall buildings without Getting A Wedgie!

TRA-LA-LAAA!

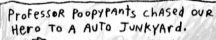

Professor Poopypants chased our Hero To A Auto JUNKYARD.

I'VE GOT you Now, WAISTBANd WARRior!

KLUNK

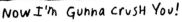

NOW I'm Gunna cRush You!

OFF

START

BIG CRUSHER Thingy 2000

CAPTAIN UnderpANTS pressed a button on his "UTILITY WAISTBAND"

"CLICK!

And out popped The Tiny ToiLet oF Truth.

CLICK

CAPTAIN UNDERPANTS Aimed The Tiny Toilet oF TRUTH AT Robo-Pippy.

B C T 2

CHAPTER 12
PROFESSOR P. GOES CRA-Z

In his entire life, Professor Poopypants had never been as angry as he was at that very moment. As he stood in the hallway, something inside his fragile brain snapped. He began shaking and sweating uncontrollably.

Suddenly, a wicked smile stretched across the professor's face. He staggered toward his empty classroom, mumbling to himself and giggling. He had hit rock bottom, and he decided to pull the rest of the planet down with him. Pippy P. Poopypants was going to take over the world!

But before I can tell you that story, I have to tell you . . . oh, never mind. I'll just tell you that story.

CHAPTER 13
HONEY, I SHRUNK THE SCHOOL

Professor Poopypants opened the storage closet in his classroom and took out the Shrinky-Pig 2000 and the Goosy-Grow 4000. He also grabbed the empty Gerbil Jogger 2000 and stumbled outside with his inventions.

The crazed professor giggled wildly to himself as he aimed the Goosy-Grow 4000 at the Gerbil Jogger 2000.

GGGGLLUUZZZZZZZZRRRRRT!

Suddenly, the Gerbil Jogger 2000 grew ten stories high.

Professor Poopypants began his long climb up the side of the giant Gerbil Jogger 2000. It took almost an hour, but eventually he reached the huge glass dome at the top and squeezed his way inside.

"Mommy?" said a little boy who was walking by with his mother. "A little old man just crawled into a giant robot suit and is about to take over a school!"

"Oh, for heaven's sake!" said his mother. "Where do you come up with this nonsense?!!? Next you'll be telling me that a giant man in his underwear is fighting the huge robot in the middle of the city!"

Professor Poopypants was now in control of the colossal Gerbil Jogger 2000. He reached down with its mighty arm, picked up the Shrinky-Pig 2000, and aimed it at the school.

BLLLLLLZZZZRRRRK!

Just then, George and Harold looked
out the window. "Hey," said George, "isn't
that the gerbil robot thingy?"

"Yeah," said Harold. "Why is it so big?"

"I don't know," said George, "but it's
getting bigger by the second!"

"Um . . ." said Harold, "I don't think it's getting bigger . . . I think *WE'RE* getting *smaller*!"

CHAPTER 14
THE PERILOUS PLOT

Professor Poopypants reached down and picked up the tiny school with his giant robotic hand. Everyone screamed in horror.

In no time at all, Eyewitness
Newswoman Ingrid Ashley was on
the scene.

"What do you want from us?" shouted
reporter Ashley.

"I want . . . a *pencil*!" screamed
Professor Poopypants.

"A pencil?!!?" asked Reporter Ashley.
"Here—take mine." She tossed a yellow
#2 pencil toward the giant robot.

Professor Poopypants reached down
with his giant robot arm, picked up
the Goosy-Grow 4000, and aimed it at
the pencil.

238

GGGGLLUUZZZZZZZZRRRRRT!

The pencil grew to the size of a tree trunk, and Professor Poopypants grabbed it.

"Follow me," he said.

The giant robot led the news crew
to the center of downtown Piqua. There,
he found three large white billboards. He
put down the Shrinky-Pig 2000 and the
Goosy-Grow 4000, and began writing on
the billboards with his giant pencil.

CHAPTER 15
THE NAME
CHANGE-O-CHART 2000

Professor Poopypants spent several
minutes jotting down a complex code
on the three giant billboards.

George and Harold, along with nearly
a thousand of their fellow shrunken
students, watched the mad professor
from the terrifying clutch of his giant
robotic hand.

"What is that crazy guy up to?" asked Mr. Krupp from his office window.

"I'LL TELL YOU," shouted Pippy Poopypants. "Everybody on the planet must now change their normal names into silly names using these three charts! Anyone who refuses will get *SHRUNK*!"

"How do the charts work?" asked Mr. Krupp.

"It's easy," said Professor Poopypants. "What's your first name?"

"Er . . . I'm not telling," said Mr. Krupp.
"WHAT IS YOUR FIRST NAME?!!?"
shouted Professor Poopypants.

"Alright, alright," said Mr. Krupp. "It's, uh . . . *Benny*." All of the children giggled.

"So the first letter of your first name is *B*," said Pippy. "Now look at the first chart and find the letter *B*."

1

FIRST CHART: USE the FirST LeTTer of YOUR FirST NAME To DeTeRMine YOUR **NEW** FirST NAME!

A= STinky
B= Lumpy
C= BuTTercup
D= Gidget
E= CRusTy
F= GReasy
G= FLuFFY
H= CheeseBall
I= Chim-Chim

J= Poopsie
K= Flunky
L= Booger
M= Pinky
N= Zippy
O= GOOBER
P= DooFus
Q= SLimy

R=LOOPY
S= Snotty
T= FALAFeL
U= DORKY
V= Squeezit
W= OpRAH
X= Skipper
Y= Dinky
Z= ZsA-ZsA

SEC
to c

A=
B=
C=
D=
E=
F=
G=
H=
I=C

Mr. Krupp looked at the chart. "It says, 'B = Lumpy,'" he whined.

"Good!" said Professor Poopypants. "Your NEW first name is '*LUMPY*!'"

All of the children laughed.

"*Lumpy* Krupp?!!?" moaned Mr. Krupp. "I don't want to be called 'Lumpy Krupp.'"

"You won't!" laughed Professor Poopypants. "Because you have to change your *last* name, too!"

"Uh-oh," said Mr. Krupp.

"Your last name is 'Krupp,'" said the professor, "which starts with a *K* and ends with a *P*. Now find the letter *K* on the second chart, and the letter *P* on the third chart."

1
FiRST CHART: USE the First Letter of YOUR FiRST NAME To DeteRmine YOUR NEW FiRST NAME!

A = StinkY
B = LumPY
C = Buttercup
D = Gidget
E = Crusty
F = Greasy
G = Fluffy
H = Cheeseball
I = Chim-Chim
J = Poopsie
K = Flunky
L = Booger
M = Pinky
N = Zippy
O = GOOBER
P = DooFus
Q = SLimy
R = LOOPY
S = Snotty
T = FALAFeL
U = DORKY
V = Squeezit
W = OPRAH
X = Skipper
Y = Dinky
Z = ZsA-ZsA

2
SEcond Chart: USE the First Letter of your Last Name to determine the First half of YOUR NEW Last Name.

A = Diaper
B = Toilet
C = Giggle
D = Bubble
E = Girdle
F = Barf
G = Lizard
H = Waffle
I = Cootie
J = Monkey
K = Potty
L = Liver
M = BANANA
N = Rhino
O = Burger
P = Hamster
Q = Toad
R = Gizzard
S = Pizza
T = Gerbil
U = Chicken
V = PickLe
W = ChuckLe
X = Tofu
Y = GoRiLLA
Z = StinkeR

ThiRd ChAR
To determ

A = HeAD
B = Mout
C = Face
D = Nose
E = Tush
F = BreAT
G = PAnts
H = Shorts
I = Lips

245

Mr. Krupp looked at the two charts.

"It says, 'K = Potty' and 'P = biscuits.'"

"Wonderful!" shouted the professor.
"Your new last name is 'Pottybiscuits.'"

"Oh, no!" groaned the principal. "My
new name is *Lumpy Pottybiscuits!*"

The children all howled with laughter.

1

FIRST CHART: USE the First Letter of YOUR FiRST NAME
To Determine YOUR NEW FiRST NAME!

A = Stinky	J = Poopsie	R = Loopy
B = Lumpy	K = Flunky	S = Snotty
C = Buttercup	L = Booger	T = FALAFeL
D = Gidget	M = Pinky	U = Dorky
E = Crusty	N = Zippy	V = Squeezit
F = Greasy	O = Goober	W = OpraH
G = Fluffy	P = DooFus	X = Skipper
H = Cheeseball	Q = SLimy	Y = Dinky
I = Chim-Chim		Z = Zsa-Zsa

2

SECOND CHART: USE the First Letter of your LAST NAME
to determine the First half of YOUR NEW LAST NAME.

A = Diaper	J = Monkey	R = Gizzard
B = Toilet	K = Potty	S = Pizza
C = Giggle	L = Liver	T = GerbiL
D = Bubble	M = BANANA	U = Chicken
E = Girdle	N = Rhino	V = Pickle
F = Barf	O = Burger	W = ChuckLe
G = Lizard	P = Hamster	X = Tofu
H = Waffle	Q = ToAd	Y = GoRiLLA
I = Cootie		Z = STinker

"Don't laugh *too* hard, kiddies," said Professor Poopypants. "You all have to change your names, too, or I'll shrink you again!"

Well, as you can imagine, nobody wanted to get shrunk *twice*! So everybody looked at the three charts and figured out their new, silly names.

3

Third Chart: Use The Last Letter of your Last Name To determine the Second half of your NEW Last Name.

A = Head
B = Mouth
C = Face
D = Nose
E = Tush
F = Breath
G = Pants
H = Shorts
I = Lips

J = Honker
K = Butt
L = Brain
M = Tushie
N = Chunks
O = Hiney
P = Biscuits
Q = Toes

R = Buns
S = Fanny
T = Sniffer
U = Sprinkles
V = Kisser
W = Squirt
X = Humperdinck
Y = Brains
Z = Juice

Stephanie Yarkoff became "Snotty Gorillabreath." Robbie Staenberg became "Loopy Pizzapants," and poor little Janet Warwick became "Poopsie Chucklebutt."

"This may be the most horrible moment in all of human history," said the local news reporter to her audience. "It seems that everyone on Earth must now change his or her name to avoid getting shrunk! Good luck to you all!

"This is Chim-Chim Diaperbrains reporting for Eyewitness News. Now, back to you, Booger."

CHAPTER 16
FLUFFY AND CHEESEBALL

This is Fluffy Toiletnose and Cheeseball Wafflefanny. Fluffy is the kid on the left with the tie and the flat-top. Cheeseball is the one on the right with the T-shirt and the bad haircut. Remember that now.

"We've got to do something," cried Fluffy.

"But what?" said Cheeseball. "We're smaller than two mice . . . what could we possibly do?"

"Let's go find our old friend, Captain Underpants!" said Fluffy.

So Fluffy and Cheeseball ran to Mr. Pottybiscuits's office and found him cowering under his desk.

"I can't believe I'm about to do this," said Fluffy, "but here goes nothing!"

Fluffy snapped his fingers.

SNAP!

Suddenly, a strange change came over
Lumpy Pottybiscuits. His worried frown
quickly turned into a heroic smile. He
rose from behind his desk and thrust out
his chest.

251

In no time at all, Mr. Pottybiscuits had removed his outer clothing and tied a red curtain around his neck.

"Tra-La-LAAAAA!" sang the hero. "Captain Underpants is here!"

"Cool!" said Cheeseball. "But from now on you have to call yourself 'Buttercup Chickenfanny.' The guy in the gerbil suit says so!"

"Hey," said Captain Underpants, "I don't take orders from *ANYBODY*!"

"Great," said Fluffy. "Now fly out that window and bring back that big machine thingy with the Lava Lamp on top."

"Yes, *SIR*," said Captain Underpants.

CHAPTER 17
CAPTAIN UNDERPANTS
TO THE RESCUE

Captain Underpants flew down to the
ground and grabbed the Goosy-Grow 4000.
But on his way back up, he was spotted by
Professor Poopypants.

The evil professor zapped Captain
Underpants with a bolt of energy from
the Shrinky-Pig 2000.

BLLLLLLZZZZRRRRK!

Suddenly, the Waistband Warrior began to shrink even *smaller* than before. He flew back to the tiny school carrying an extremely small Goosy-Grow 4000, and he dropped it into Fluffy's hand.

"Hey, where's Captain Underpants?" asked Fluffy.

"I don't know," said Cheeseball. "I think he got shrunk so small that we can't see him anymore."

"Well," said Fluffy, "at least we have this little invention thingy."

"How's that going to help us?" asked Cheeseball.

"I saw Professor Poopypants use it to make that pencil grow really big," said Fluffy. "It's our only hope of ever getting back to normal size!"

"I hope it still works," said Cheeseball.

Fluffy and Cheeseball dashed to the school kitchen and climbed up the ladder onto the roof.

"Maybe if we zap the school with this thing, everybody will grow back to normal size," said Fluffy.

"Good idea," said Cheeseball. "Then we can all run away!"

CHAPTER 18
ARE YOU THERE, GOD? IT'S US, FLUFFY AND CHEESEBALL

Fluffy pointed the Goosy-Grow 4000 at the roof of the school and got ready to press the button. But the boys were spotted by Professor Poopypants. Quickly, he turned his mighty robotic hand, and Fluffy and Cheeseball slid off the roof. Downward they tumbled through the air.

"Oh, NO," shouted Cheeseball. "We're DOOMED!"

"Wait a second," cried Fluffy. "Do you have a piece of paper on you?"

"Yeah," screamed Cheeseball. "Right here in my pocket. But what good is it gonna do us now?"

"Quick!" cried Fluffy. "Fold it into a paper airplane!"

"What *kind* of paper airplane?" asked Cheeseball.

"ANY KIND!" screamed Fluffy. "JUST DO IT NOW!"

Quickly, Cheeseball folded the paper into a goofy-looking glider. "How's this?" he screamed.

"Great!" yelled Fluffy. "Now hold it steady!" Fluffy pointed the tiny Goosy-Grow 4000 at Cheeseball's airplane, and he pressed the button.

GGGGLLUUZZZZZZZZZRRRRRT!

Suddenly, Cheeseball's airplane grew to an enormous size. Fluffy and Cheeseball flopped down into it, and the paper airplane took off, gliding through the air.

"Oh, MAN!" cried Cheeseball. "I can't believe that worked!"

"We're not out of this yet!" yelled Fluffy.

CHAPTER 19
THE FLIGHT OF
THE GOOFY GLIDER

Fluffy and Cheeseball had to admit that it was pretty cool flying over the city streets on a paper airplane. They didn't even seem to mind the fact that they were only about an inch tall each.

But you can probably imagine the boys' concern when they started heading straight for a wood chipper.

"Oh, NO!" cried Fluffy. "We're gonna get, um . . . *WOOD CHIPPERED* to death!"

Cheeseball couldn't look. He put his hands over his eyes and waited for the inevitable.

But suddenly, *SWOOOOSH!* The paper airplane swerved sharply and missed the wood chipper altogether.

"Hey!" cried Fluffy. "How did that happen?"

"I don't know," said Cheeseball. "*I'm* not steering this thing!"

The boys had barely caught their breath
when a small dog noticed the airplane and
came running after them.

"Oh, NO!" cried Cheeseball. "We're
gonna get eaten by a *WIENER DOG*!"

Fluffy covered *his* eyes this time.

But wouldn't you know it, the airplane
swerved sharply upward and out of the
range of the little dog altogether.

"Are you doing that?" asked Cheeseball.

"No," said Fluffy. "It must be the wind!"

Finally, the paper airplane landed in a wet, sticky pile of hot blacktop.

"Yuck!" said Fluffy. "What could be worse than gettin' stuck in a pile of *blacktop*?"

"Maybe getting crushed by a big steamroller thingy," said Cheeseball.

"You sure have an active imagination," said Fluffy.

"No, I don't," said Cheeseball, as he pointed upward. "*Look!*"

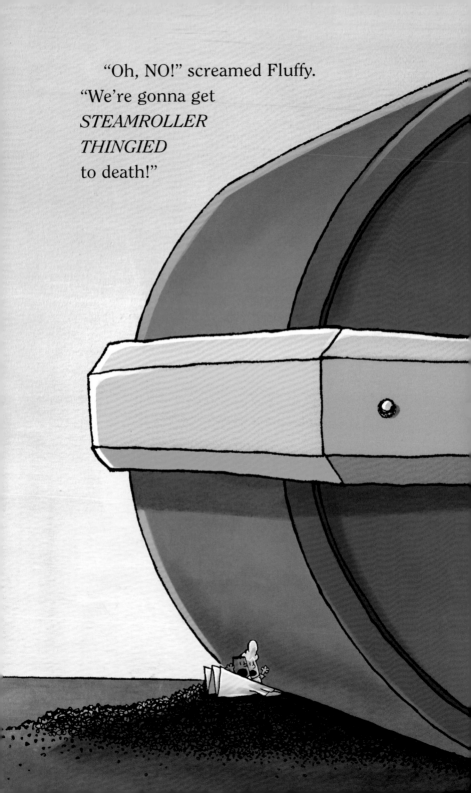

"Oh, NO!" screamed Fluffy.
"We're gonna get
STEAMROLLER
THINGIED
to death!"

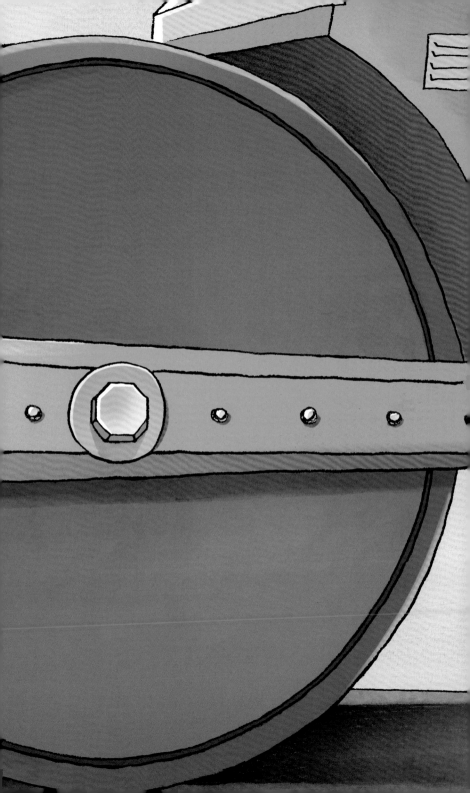

Just then, the boys were yanked up by the backs of their shirts and carried off through the air to safety.

"Something's got a hold of us!" cried Cheeseball. "But I can't see what it is!"

"It must be Captain Underpants," said Fluffy. "We just can't see him because he's so small!"

"Hey," said Cheeseball, "I'll bet he was steering the airplane out of danger, too!"

"*OUR HERO!*" the boys shouted.

CHAPTER 20
X-TRA, X-TRA, X-TRA, X-TRA, X-TRA, X-TRA, X-TRA, X-TRA, X-TRA LARGE UNDERPANTS

Fluffy and Cheeseball landed safely in an abandoned alley.

"We've got to enlarge Captain Underpants so he can fight Professor Poopypants," said Fluffy. "The fate of the entire planet is in our hands!"

"But how can we enlarge him if we can't even see him?" asked Cheeseball.

"Good question," said Fluffy.

"Wait," said Cheeseball. "I've got an
idea." He called out as loud as he could:
"Captain Underpants! We can't see you,
but if you can hear us, fly over and land
on my finger. We have a machine that can
make you big again."

The boys waited a few seconds.

"Look, Fluffy!" said Cheeseball. "There
he is! See? He's that little tiny speck on
my finger. Now just aim the machine at that
little speck . . . but don't zap my finger, OK?"

"Don't worry," said Fluffy. "I'm a great
shot with this thing. I won't zap your . . ."

GGGGLLUUZZZZZZZZRRRRRT!

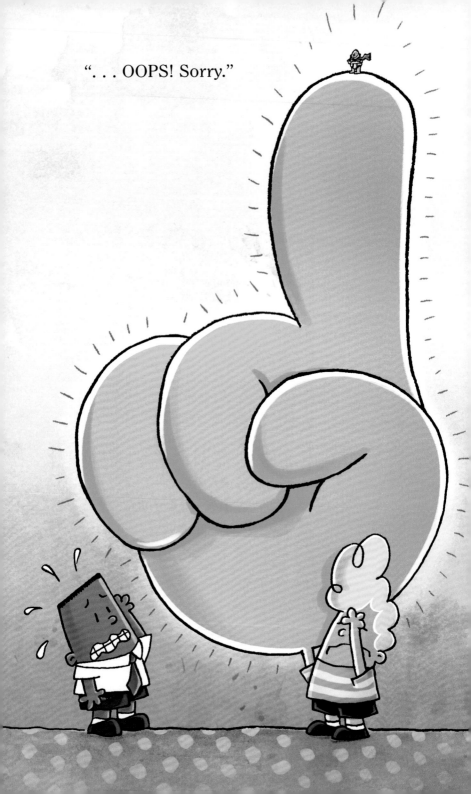

The good news was that Captain
Underpants had grown larger and was now
visible. The bad news was, well, let's just
say that Cheeseball was going to have an
awful hard time picking his nose with his
right hand from now on.

Fluffy gave Captain Underpants a few
more shots from the Goosy-Grow 4000.
The Waistband Warrior grew and grew
and grew until he was ten stories high.

Finally, the colossal captain headed toward the preposterous professor. A showdown was about to begin.

The little boy from chapter 13 happened to be walking by with his mother again. He looked up and saw a giant man in his underwear getting ready to fight a huge robot in the middle of the city.

"Mommy?" said the little boy.

"What?" asked his mother.

"Umm . . . never mind," said the boy.

CHAPTER 21
THE INCREDIBLY GRAPHIC VIOLENCE CHAPTER
(IN FLIP-O-RAMA™)

WARNING:

The following chapter contains scenes that are so intense and horrific, they may not be suitable for viewing by people who can't take a joke.

If you are easily offended, or if you tend to blame all of society's evils on TV shows and cartoon characters, please run to your nearest supermarket and get a life. They're located in the "Get Real" section next to the clues.

Good luck!

PILKEY® BRAND

‑RAMA

HERE'S HOW IT WORKS!

STEP 1

First, place your *left* hand inside the dotted lines marked "LEFT HAND HERE." Hold the book open *flat*.

STEP 2

Grasp the *right-hand* page with your right thumb and index finger (inside the dotted lines marked "RIGHT THUMB HERE").

STEP 3

Now *quickly* flip the right-hand page back and forth until the picture appears to be *animated*.

(For extra fun, try adding your own sound-effects!)

FLIP-O-RAMA 1

(pages 279 and 281)

Remember, flip *only* page 279.
While you are flipping, be sure you
can see the picture on page 279
and the one on page 281.
If you flip quickly, the two
pictures will start to look like
<u>one</u> *animated* picture.

Don't forget to
add your own sound-effects!

LEFT HAND HERE

PROFESSOR POOPYPANTS PACKED A POWERFUL PUNCH!

279

RIGHT
THUMB
HERE

PROFESSOR POOPYPANTS PACKED A POWERFUL PUNCH!

FLIP-O-RAMA 2

(pages 283 and 285)

Remember, flip *only* page 283.
While you are flipping, be sure you
can see the picture on page 283
and the one on page 285.
If you flip quickly, the two
pictures will start to look like
<u>one</u> *animated* picture.

Don't forget to
add your own sound-effects!

LEFT HAND HERE

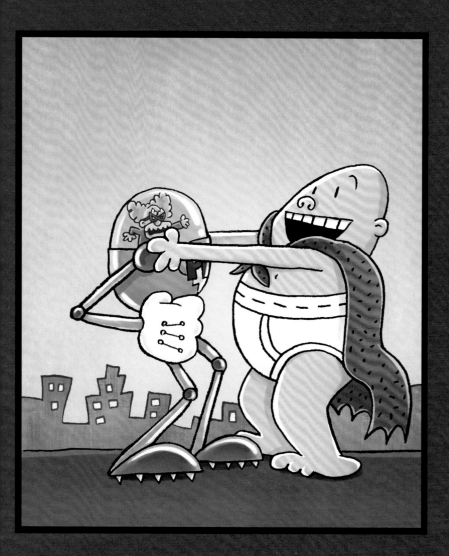

BUT THE HEAD-BUTTIN' HERO HALTED THE HORROR!

RIGHT
THUMB
HERE

284

BUT THE HEAD-BUTTIN'
HERO HALTED THE
HORROR!

FLIP-O-RAMA 3

(pages 287 and 289)

Remember, flip *only* page 287.
While you are flipping, be sure you
can see the picture on page 287
and the one on page 289.
If you flip quickly, the two
pictures will start to look like
<u>one</u> *animated* picture.

Don't forget to
add your own sound-effects!

LEFT HAND HERE

THE BRIEF-WEARIN' BANDIT BATTLED THE BIONIC BEHEMOTH!

287

RIGHT THUMB HERE

RIGHT
INDEX
FINGER
HERE

288

THE BRIEF-WEARIN'
BANDIT BATTLED THE
BIONIC BEHEMOTH!

FLIP-O-RAMA 4

(pages 291 and 293)

Remember, flip *only* page 291.
While you are flipping, be sure you
can see the picture on page 291
and the one on page 293.
If you flip quickly, the two
pictures will start to look like
<u>one</u> *animated* picture.

Don't forget to
add your own sound-effects!

LEFT HAND HERE

THE WAISTBAND
WARRIOR WON
THE WAR!

291

RIGHT
THUMB
HERE

RIGHT
INDEX
FINGER
HERE

292

THE WAISTBAND
WARRIOR WON
THE WAR!

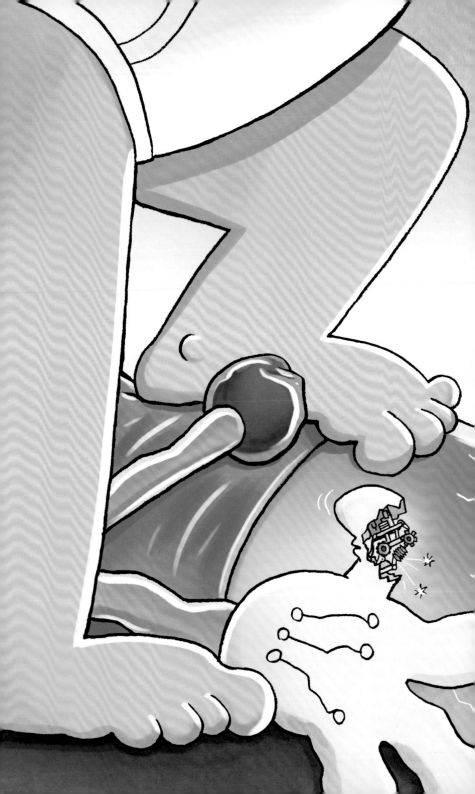

CHAPTER 22
THE TWENTY-SECOND CHAPTER

Professor Poopypants had been defeated, and everybody in the school cheered wildly. They were still small, but at least they got their old names back.

"I'm sure glad I don't have a silly name anymore," said Ms. Ribble.

"Me, too," said Mr. Rected.

"Hooray!" cried George. "Let's all give Captain Underpants a big *hand*!"

Harold was not amused.

"Oops . . ." said George. "Sorry."

"That's OK," said Harold. "Just gimme that invention thing so I can zap us back to normal!"

TAP
TAP
TAP

Harold held the Goosy-Grow 4000 in
his giant hand and zapped George and
himself (that is, every part of himself
EXCEPT his giant hand).

GGGGLLUUZZZZZZZZRRRRRT!

Suddenly, George and Harold were back to their normal sizes again.

"Boy," said George, "we sure have tested the limits of science today!"

"Yep!" said Harold. "*And* the limits of our readers' willing suspension of disbelief!"

"Er . . . *yyyeah*," said George, "that, too!"

George and Harold picked up their tiny school and carried it back to where it belonged. George got ready to zap the school with the Goosy-Grow 4000, while Harold prepared to zap Captain Underpants with the Shrinky-Pig 2000.

"I sure hope this works," said George.

"Me, too," said Harold.

CHAPTER 23
TO MAKE A
LONG STORY
SHORT

It did.

CHAPTER 24
THE CHAPTER BEFORE
THE LAST CHAPTER

George took Captain Underpants over to
the bushes behind the school and ordered
him to dress back up like Mr. Krupp.

"Let's go, bub," said George. "We
haven't got all day!"

Then Harold had some fun with the
garden hose. In no time at all, Mr. Krupp
was back to his old nasty self again.

Soon the cops showed up to arrest Professor Poopypants.

"There's one thing I don't understand," said George to the professor. "Wouldn't it have been *smarter* to change *your own name* instead of forcing the rest of the world to change theirs?"

"Gosh," said Professor Poopypants, "I never thought of that!"

302

A few weeks later, George and Harold received a letter from the Piqua State Penitentiary.

PIQUA STATE PEN.

A NICE PLACE TO VISIT
... BUT YOU WOULDN'T WANT TO LIVE HERE.

Dear George and Harold,

Sorry about trying to overthrow the world and everything. I've decided to take your advice and change my name so that people won't laugh at me anymore.

From now on I'll be going by my Grandfather's name (on my mother's side). It's such a relief knowing that nobody will ever make fun of my name again.

Signed,
Tippy Tinkletrousers

CHAPTER 25
THE CHAPTER AFTER
THE CHAPTER BEFORE
THE LAST CHAPTER

"You know," said George, "I really learned something today."

"What's that?" asked Harold.

"I learned that it's not nice to make fun of people," said George.

"Wow," said Harold. "I think this is the first time one of our stories ever had a *moral*!"

"Probably the last time, too," said George.

"Let's hope so," said Harold.

But George and Harold had forgotten
all about the *other* moral they had learned
along the way, which was: "Don't ever,
ever, *EVER* hypnotize your principal."
Because if you do, your life can go
from bad to worse . . .

. . . at the *snap* of a finger!

"OH, NO!" screamed Harold.
"HERE WE GO AGAIN!" screamed
George.

FUN FACTS

FUN FACT #1

This book began as a title. Dav thought
of it one day while he was sitting in a
movie theater waiting for the previews
to start. The title itself was really funny,
but Dav knew he didn't want to write a
story about a guy with poop in his pants.
(Believe it or not, even Dav has his limits!)
Dav wondered, "What if he just had a silly
name? What if he was a really smart guy
who was just cursed with a funny name?
I began to think of Albert Einstein, who
was a true genius. But what if his name
had been Stinky Girdlechunks? Would
anybody have taken him seriously?" Dav
wrote the rest of the story to find out.

FUN FACT #2

Although Professor Poopypants's name
makes everyone laugh, Dav didn't want
his book to promote name-calling. Growing
up, Dav was teased because of his last name.
Kids called him "Dav Pinky" and "Dav
Pickles" and even "Dav Puke-y" — all
because of the last name he was born with.

But what if you could take anybody's given name, regardless if it was funny or not, and insert it into an equation that would make *everybody's* name equally ridiculous? That's how the Name Change-O-Chart 2000 came to be. Now a kid named Larry Drake would no longer be able to make fun of a kid named Johnny Butts, because Booger Bubbletush is just as silly a name as Poopsie Toiletfanny.

FUN FACT #3

One of Dav's picture-book characters makes a guest appearance in this book. Can you spot him? (Hint: His last name is "Myers.")

FUN FACT #4

Professor Poopypants is loosely modeled on Albert Einstein, who was the inspiration for this character. The real Einstein was much taller though — five feet and nine inches.

FUN FACT #5

In the original edition of this book, the logo for Piqua State Penitentiary in the letter on page 303 contained an error. Dav used the abbreviation "Penn." This is all somebody else's fault, and has nothing to do with the ugly rumor that Dav Pilkey doesn't know how to spell *penitentiary*.

Professor Poopypants' Name Change-O-Chart 2000

No one laughs at Professor Pippy P. Poopypants and gets away with it. Find out what your new name is with my nasty Name Change-O-Chart 2000, or face the wrath of the Shrinky-Pig 2000!

FIRST CHART: USE the First Letter of Your First Name To Determine Your NEW First NAME!

A= Stinky	J= Poopsie	R= Loopy
B = Lumpy	K= Flunky	S= Snotty
C= Buttercup	L= Booger	T= Falafel
D= Gidget	M= Pinky	U= Dorky
E= Crusty	N= Zippy	V= Squeezit
F= Greasy	O= Goober	W= Oprah
G= Fluffy	P= Doofus	X= Skipper
H= Cheeseball	Q= Slimy	Y= Dinky
I= Chim-Chim		Z= Zsa-Zsa

2

SECOND CHART: USE the first Letter of your LAST NAME to determine the FIRST half of your **NEW** Last Name.

A= Diaper
B= Toilet
C= Giggle
D= Bubble
E= Girdle
F= Barf
G= Lizard
H= Waffle
I= Cootie

J= Monkey
K= Potty
L= Liver
M= BANANA
N= Rhino
O= Burger
P= Hamster
Q= Toad

R= Gizzard
S= Pizza
T= Gerbil
U= Chicken
V= Pickle
W= Chuckle
X= Tofu
Y= GoRiLLA
Z= Stinker

3

Third CHART: Use The LAST Letter of your LAST NAME To determine the Second half of your **NEW** Last Name.

A= Head
B= Mouth
C= Face
D= Nose
E= Tush
F= Breath
G= PAnts
H= Shorts
I= Lips

J= Honker
K= Butt
L= Brain
M= Tushie
N= Chunks
O= Hiney
P= Biscuits
Q= Toes

R= Buns
S= FAnny
T= Sniffer
U= Sprinkles
V= Kisser
W= Squirt
X= Humperdinck
Y= BrAins
Z= Juice

NOW AVAILABLE

The Graphic Novel that Started it all!

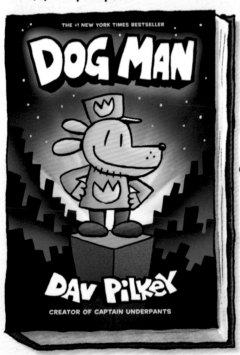

When we were in kindergarten, we made up our first Hero Ever: Dog Man!

me too!

Now Dog Man Stars in his own Full-Length Graphic Novel Series!!!

So WAG Your Tails and Howl at the MOON...

The Adventures of DOG MAN Are ready For You!!!

From George and Harold

Get ready for action...

...Suspense...

...Romance...

sniff

SNIFF

...and Laffs!

Laugh Your tails off!!!

DOG MAN

Read it to Your dog!!!

and then...

DOGMAN

Fetch Your copy soon!!!

mBLFF!

DOG MAN

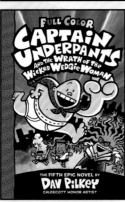

TH DAV PILKEY!

ABOUT THE
AUTHOR-ILLUSTRATOR

When Dav Pilkey was a kid, he was diagnosed with ADHD and dyslexia. Dav was so disruptive in class that his teachers made him sit out in the hallway every day. Luckily, Dav loved to draw and make up stories. He spent his time in the hallway creating his own original comic books — the very first adventures of Dog Man and Captain Underpants.

In college, Dav met a teacher who encouraged him to illustrate and write. He won a national competition in 1986 and the prize was the publication of his first book, WORLD WAR WON. He made many other books before being awarded the 1998 California Young Reader Medal for DOG BREATH, which was published in 1994, and in 1997 he won the Caldecott Honor for THE PAPERBOY.

THE ADVENTURES OF SUPER DIAPER BABY, published in 2002, was the first complete graphic novel spin-off from the Captain Underpants series and appeared at #6 on the USA Today bestseller list for all books, both adult and children's, and was also a New York Times bestseller. It was followed by THE ADVENTURES OF OOK AND GLUK: KUNG FU CAVEMEN FROM THE FUTURE and SUPER DIAPER BABY 2: THE INVASION OF THE POTTY SNATCHERS, both USA Today bestsellers. The unconventional style of these graphic novels is intended to encourage uninhibited creativity in kids.

His stories are semi-autobiographical and explore universal themes that celebrate friendship, tolerance, and the triumph of the good-hearted.

Dav loves to kayak in the Pacific Northwest with his wife.